Marco's Run

Marco's Run

Wesley Cartier

Illustrated by Reynold Ruffins

Green Light Readers
Harcourt, Inc.
San Diego   New York   London

Requests for permission to make copies of any part of the work should be mailed
to the following address: Permissions Department, Harcourt, Inc.,
6277 Sea Harbor Drive, Orlando, Florida 32887-6777.

www.harcourt.com

First Green Light Readers edition 2001
Green Light Readers is a trademark of Harcourt, Inc.,
registered in the United States of America and/or other jurisdictions.

Library of Congress Cataloging-in-Publication Data
Cartier, Wesley.
Marco's run/by Wesley Cartier; illustrated by Reynold Ruffins.
p. cm.
"Green Light Readers."
Summary: A boy runs so fast that he imagines himself to be a rabbit, a bobcat, a horse,
and a cheetah.
[1. Running—Fiction. 2. Speed—Fiction. 3. Imagination—Fiction. 4. Animals—
Fiction.] I. Ruffins, Reynold, ill. II. Title. III. Green Light reader.
PZ7.C2485Mar 2001
[E]—dc21   00-9727
ISBN 0-15-216243-7
ISBN 0-15-216249-6 (pb)

A C E G H F D B
A C E G H F D B (pb)

It's time for a run in the park.

As I run, I think, I must be fast.
I wish I could run like…

…a rabbit!

A rabbit hops through the grass.
He's kicking with his long back
legs. Off he goes.

I run like that rabbit.

I hop and kick. Then I think,
I must be fast. I wish I could
run like…

…a bobcat!

A bobcat runs on the forest path.
She darts off in a flash to hunt.

I run like that bobcat.

I rush down the park path. Then
I think, I must be very fast. I wish
I could run like…

…a horse!

A horse starts with a trot. Then, all of a sudden, she takes off like the wind!

I run like that horse.

The wind swishes past me. Then
I think, I must be the fastest of all.
I wish I could run like…

...a cheetah!

A swift cheetah flashes by.
No one can catch him!

I run like that cheetah.

Then, I am huffing and puffing!
I can't run anymore. Now I wish
I were…

…back home.

I huff and puff and
sit down with a *thump*.

Then I think…

NOW I NEED A REST!

Meet the Illustrator

Reynold Ruffins loves to draw. He says, "Drawing can be a great adventure!" Drawing gives him the chance to show things that no one has ever thought of. "I like to show that pictures can tell a story just the way words do," he says.

© 1999 Todd Bigelow/Black Star

Reynold Ruffins